Fire Proves Iron ™

grounded stars

Story
Page Malbrough

Art
Michael C. Malbrough

with Inks by
G.W. Fisher

Production Assistance
Ann Gel Fairlie
Konrad Michelsen

Additional Concept Design
Jong Kim
Jason Baroody

Logo Design
Jason Just
Michael C. Malbrough

Fire Proves Iron created by
Page Malbrough
Michael C. Malbrough

fonts by www.blambot.com

WWW.FIREPROVESIRON.COM

"…a town of unnatural red and black like the painted face of a savage. It was a town of machinery and tall chimneys, out of which interminable serpents of smoke trailed themselves for ever and ever, and never got uncoiled…vast piles of buildings full of windows where there was a rattling and a trembling all day long, and where the piston of the steam-engine worked monotonously up and down, like the head of an elephant in a state of melancholy madness…"

Charles Dickens
Hard Times

THE PRECARIAN RACE — A PEOPLE OF INCREDIBLE METAMORPHOSIS.

AS SKILLED PIONEERS, WE EMBRACED PROGRESS.

AS EXPLORERS, WE BUILT INTRICATE MACHINES THAT BURROWED
INTO THE DEEP.

AND AS INVENTORS, IT WAS IN THIS UNTOUCHED SOIL
THAT WE FIRST DISCOVERED THE MINERAL THAT
OFFERS NEW LIFE...

A LIFE WHERE ONLY THE MECHAN THRIVES.

I HAVE BUILT US OUR VERY OWN CITY,
A MEGALOPOLIS, WHERE NEW GENERATIONS ARE REVOLUTIONIZED
INTO A TRUE SELF. AS FOR SKIMPS, OUR FLAWED PREDECESSORS,
THEIR FUNCTION IS ONE OF TAXING LABOR AND AGONIZING EFFORT.
BUT FROM DUST THEY WERE RAISED AND TO DUST THEY WILL RETURN.

THEN ONCE AND FOR ALL, WE'LL LEAVE BEHIND OUR
ATAVISTIC HALVES.

WE CALL OUR CITY...

...NEW PROMISE.

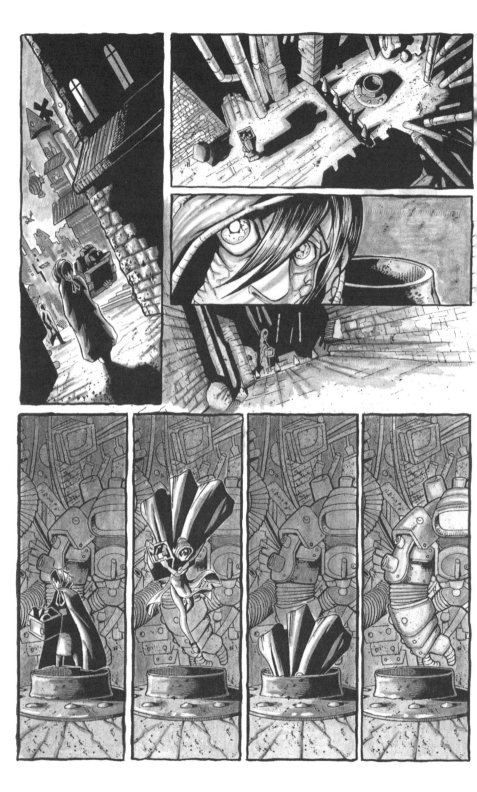

Will not these grounded stars

cursed to   plummet   and   shatter

crumble into

dust

of

finer

matter?

Birthright

Between juts of craggy briar,
hangs the smoke of furnace fire.
Metal chinks above the drone
as pipesound prattles off a stone.
Twisting gear, cog and wheel
turning clay, bone and steel
around mineral men and tyrant
slave, spirit, giant
but in a shaft of silence
                a man's soul unfolds.

Below
cloud and grime
where mirrors reflect
only the night,
in the city
cut into a thousand sides,
like a sullied prism
void of light---
                a man's soul unfolds.

He calls into its chasm
again and again.
Each resounding word
lifts beyond the clatter,
strikes
and catches on the air
newly born.

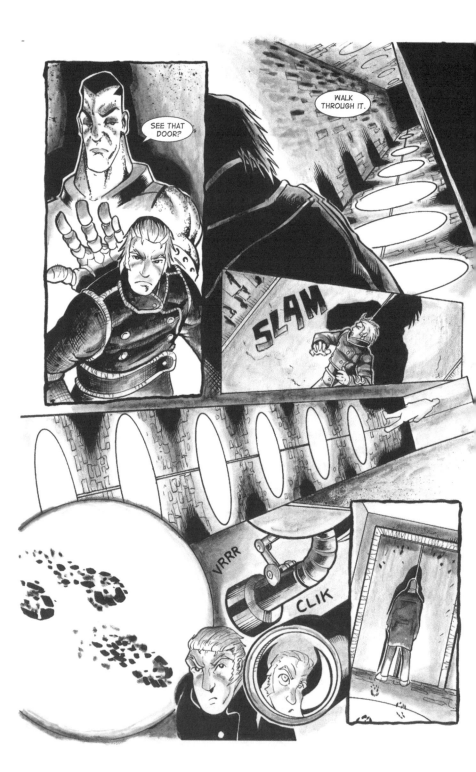

TUK, TUK, TUK...NO IGREMIOUS, IT'S LIKE I'VE BEEN TELLING YOU.
YOU'RE MISSING THE POINT.
THINK OF ALL THE POSSIBILITIES.

MY SWOOPER COMPLETELY BLEW THIS MORNING.
A HUNK CAME OFF WHILE I WAS
TRYING THE ENGINE...WHERE CAN I FIND
A BAG OF JIBBERNAUGHTS?

grumblegrumblegrumblegrumblegrumblegrumblegrumble

OH, MY MOTHER IS GORGEOUS...HER EYES GLIMMER LIKE WATER AND HER SKIN'S AS
HARD AS DIAMONDS...WOULDN'T YOU KNOW I TOOK AFTER MY FATHER'S SIDE...HE
LOOKS LIKE A LUMP OF WET CLAY WITH EYEHOLES...URRGH, SHE'LL OUTLIVE US ALL.

HIS KIND SHOULDN'T BE WALKING AROUND AIMLESSLY.
WHEN WILL THEY BE OVER
WITH ANYWAY?
ARE YOU GOING? SHOULD BE QUITE IMPRESSIVE...
THIS CHILD'S FAMILY WAS ONE OF
THE FIRST TO ARRIVE...BACK AT THE CITY'S INCEPTION.

AAAH...

FENNEL WILL BE SURE
TO MAKE AN APPEARANCE...

HAA! HAA! HAA!

FILTHY, DIRTY WENDELS...

IF THRID HAD ANY SENSE, IT WOULD CHAR EVERYTHING DOWN BELOW. NO
RESPECTABLE CREATURE WOULD DARE TO LIVE IN SUCH STIFLING CONDITIONS.

A RIGOROUS DOSE OF GENUINE CORE AVAILABLE TO THE MASSES...ONLY HERE
FIND IT NOWHERE ELSE!

OH VARM, I CAN'T SEEM TO GET HIS ATTENTION. STAGS!

snap! snap!

HEY YOU!!! UP THERE!

snap! snap!   STAGS, I'M TALKING TO YOU!!!

REMAIN IN THE C...

EX

JIB JIB

GET CUT

PROPRIETY WEST END.

WHY AM I DOING THIS?

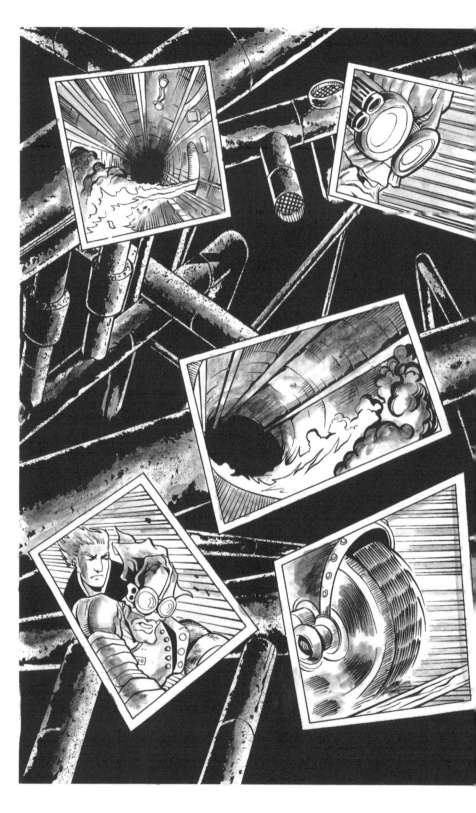

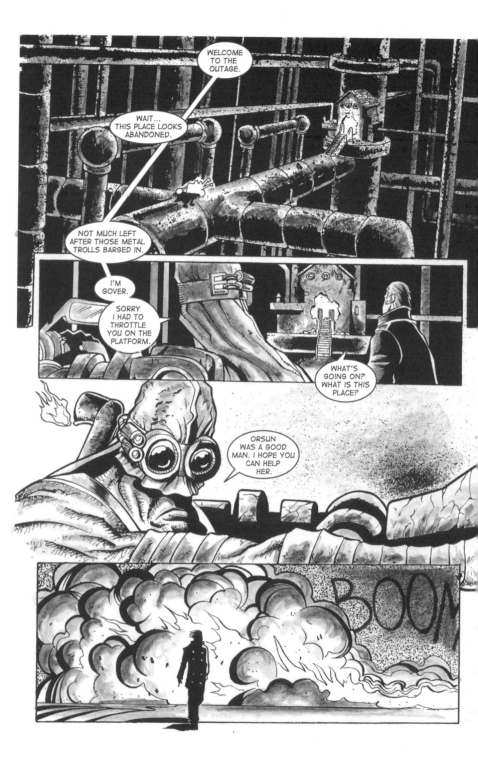

beckoned into a wilderness towards the echos of his own steps.

I FOLLOWED THE TRAIL OF YOUR INEPTITUDE.

IT'S PATHETIC WHEN YOU SKIMPS TRY TO ESCAPE THE LIFE *YOU* CHOSE.

I'M NOT GOING BACK UP.

GOOD FOR YOU.

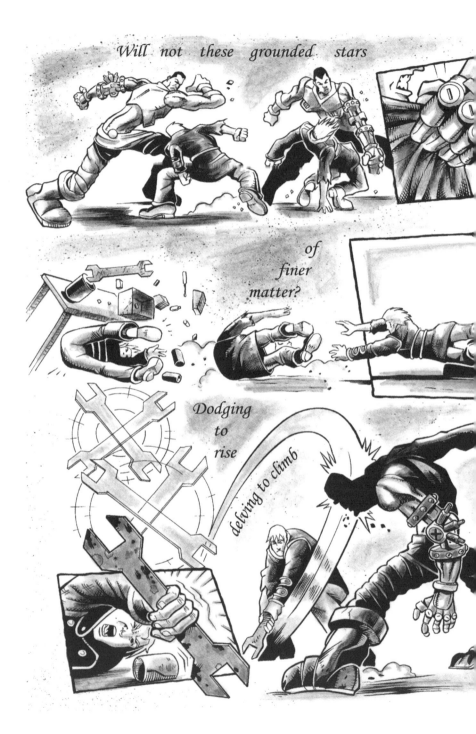

light burning,
light blinding

light breathing.

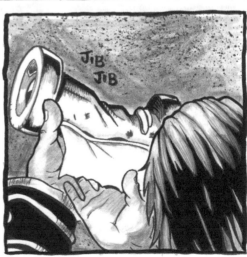

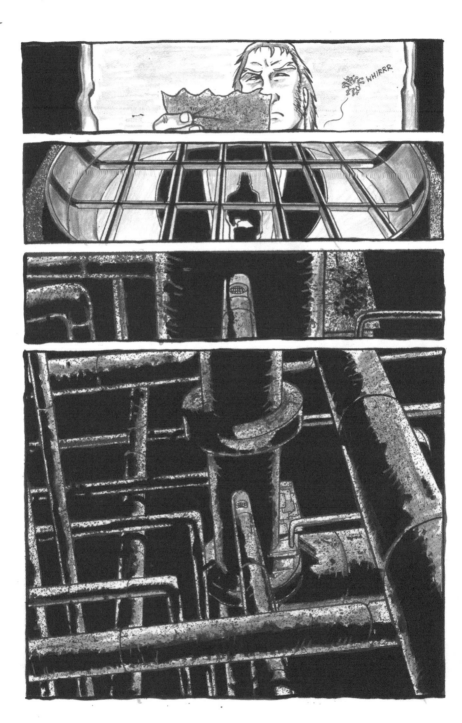

Amalgam of Man, Mineral, and Machine...

The Precarian race, a people split into two ranks:
the Mechan, a mysterious amalgam of mineral, machine and man
who has enslaved the more inferior class, better known as the
"skimp" population.

FIRE PROVES IRON deals largely with stereotypical perceptions of truth, power and purpose and the comic book art form ideally approaches such a subject because it's a genre that is itself stereotyped and easily tossed off as a childish, violent, sexist, bad art display for the simpleminded overrun with clichés and one dimensional characters. This story looks at a people with their own history who need their humanity restored---that individualism that can emerge only from the depth apparent in human struggle and toil.

That individual voice makes poetry so integral to this story by allowing windows of opportunity for readers amidst the explosion of artwork on the page. By slowing down the plot, the poems allow time for reflection, not to repeat with words what is already there visually, but to encourage going beyond the page into one's own imagination. Here, the reader is free to question and build upon what the art already generously offers.

How does what civilization creates affect humanity quite literally from the inside out? How do machines change the landscape and what is truly relevant in an age of technology? How does industry affect our outer appearances and our inner souls? For the sake of efficiency, must man lose his humanity? Our machines are breeders unable to function without moving forward. When a person is tied to the tracks, the train is incapable of stopping, but must continue on its course and take his life...that is, unless someone else happens to come along...

Thank you to our family and friends who have supported this project and to our Creator who has enabled us the desire and the ability to create.   -Page and Michael

No man is an island: Thanks to my wife Fran, daughters Stephanie, Keri, & Jessica, sisters Debbie, Linda, & Donna, and especially to my father Glen; through your love, patience, & support I've become the man I am today. Thanks also to Page & Mike for letting me play in their yard with all these really neat toys.

This work is dedicated to our Lord and Savior Jesus Christ, who is preparing a room for me in His Father's house; and to my late mother Geneva, who as I write this is undoubtedly cleaning it.   -G.W. Fisher 4/5/04